Put Me in the Zoo

by Robert Lopshire

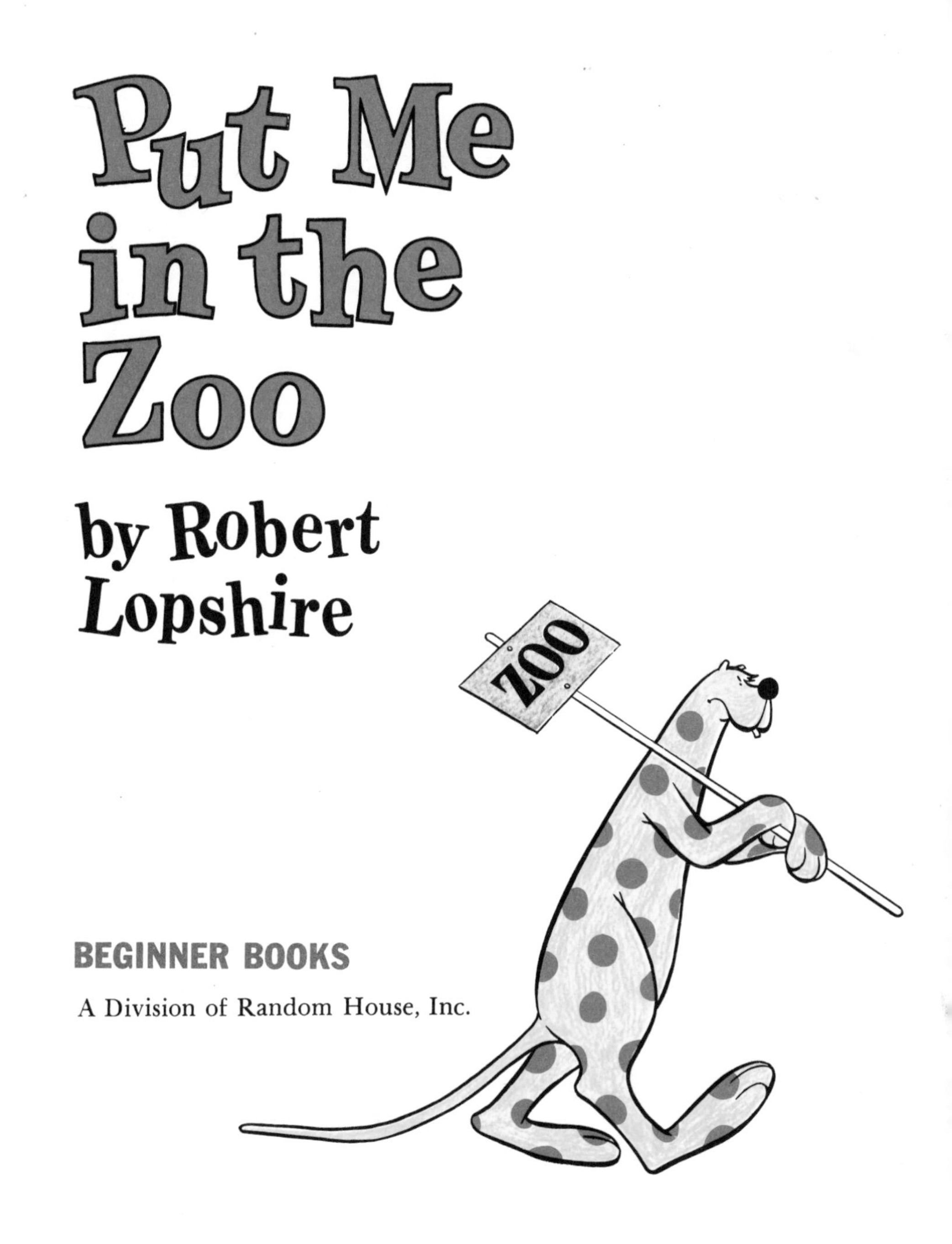

BEGINNER BOOKS

A Division of Random House, Inc.

PUT ME IN THE ZOO

This title was originally catalogued by the Library of Congress as follows: Lopshire, Robert. Put me in the zoo. [New York] Beginner Books: distributed by Random House [1960] 58 p. illus. 24 cm. (Beginner books, B–17) I. Title PZ8.3.L862Pu 60–13494 ISBN 0-394-80017-6 ISBN 0-394-90017-0 (lib. bdg.)

 Published in New York by Beginner Books, Inc., and simultaneously in Toronto, Canada, by Random House of Canada Limited. Manufactured in the United States of America. 116

To Ted, Helen and Phyllis

I will go into the zoo.

I want to see it.

Yes, I do.

ZOO

I would like to
live this way.
This is where
I want to stay.

Will you keep me
in the zoo?
I want to stay
in here with you.

ZOO

We do not want you
in the zoo.
Out you go!
Out! Out with you.

ZO
ZO

Why did they
put me out this way?
I should be in.
I want to stay.

ZOO

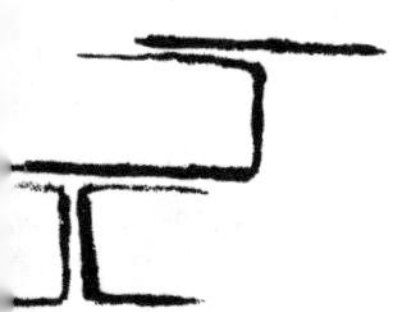

Why should they
put you in the zoo?
What good are you?
What can you do?

What good am I?
What can I do?
Now here is one thing
I can do.

Look! Now all his spots
are blue!

And now his spots are orange!

Say!

He looks very good

that way.

Now look at this!

What do you see?

Green spots! As green
as green can be!

Violet spots!
Say! You are good!
Do more! Do more!
We wish you would.

I can do more.
Look! This is new.
Blue, orange, green,
and violet, too.

Oh! They would put me
in the zoo,
if they could see
what I can do.

I can put my spots
up on this ball.

And I can put them

on a wall.

I can put them
on a cat
And I can put them
on a hat.

I can put them
on the zoo!

And I can put
my spots on you!

Look at this, now!

One! Two! Three!

I can put them
on a tree.

And now
when I say “One, two, three”

All my spots
are back on me!

Look, now!
Here is one thing more.
I take my spots.
I make them four.

Oh! They would put me
in the zoo,
if they could see
what I can do.

I take my spots,
I take them all,

And I can make them
very small.

And now, you see,
I take them all
and I can make them
very tall.

And when I want
to have more fun,
I take my spots
and make them one.

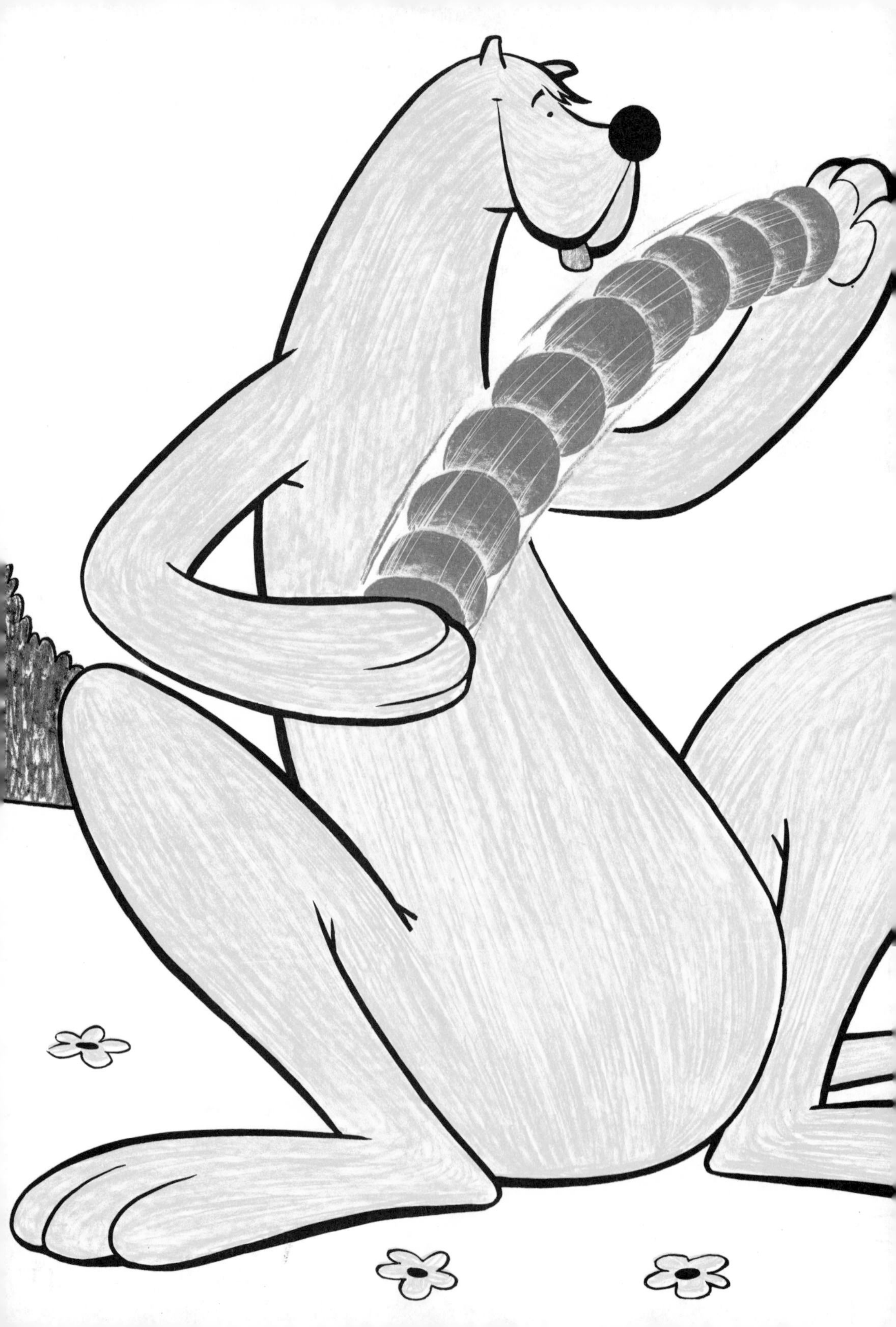

Yes, they should put me
in the zoo.
The things my spots
and I can do!

See! I can put them
in a box.

ZOO

I take them out.

They look like socks.

And I can put them
way up high.
Up, up they go!
I make them fly.

I put them
high up in the air.
My spots fly here.
My spots fly there.

I call them back, now,

One! Two! Three!

Now all my spots
are back with me.
Tell me. Tell me, now,
you two.
Do you like
the things I do?

Tell me. Tell me, now,
you two.
Will they put me
in the zoo?

We like all
the things you do.
We like your spots,
we like you, too.

But
you should not
be in the zoo.
No. You should NOT
be in the zoo.

With all the things
that you can do,
the circus
is the place
for you!

Yes!
This is where
I want to be.
The circus is
the place for me!